The nightmare
is just beginning . . .

Glancing in his rearview mirror, John Loengard froze. A strong, bright light flashed in the mirror, then was gone. Loengard quickly craned his neck around to peer out the rear window. Nothing.

He turned to look at the road again, and there it was, dead ahead: a strange black craft hovering in the sky.

The sick feeling in Loengard's stomach turned to terror as a beam of light burst from the thing, piercing the darkness. The light searched for and found its target—Loengard's car.

dark skies™

Book 1: The Awakening

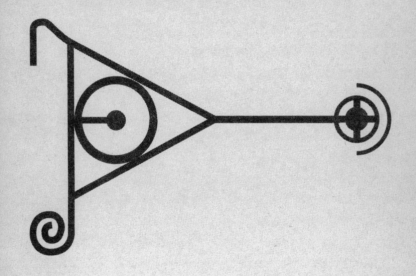

dark skies™

Book 1: The Awakening

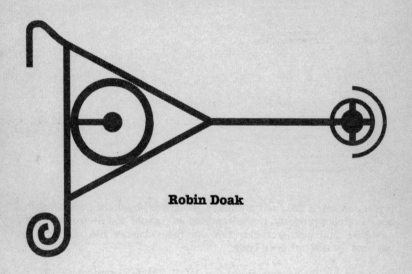

Robin Doak

Published by Troll Communications L.L.C. TM & Copyright © 1997 by Columbia Pictures Television, Inc.

Printed in the United States of America.

10 9 8 7 6 5 4 3 2 1

dark skies™

Book 1: The Awakening

Chapter 1

July 1960
White Mountains, New Hampshire

Betty Hill looked out the open car window at the trees and fields flying by and tried to stifle a yawn. She and her husband, Barney, had about two hours left to drive. She wanted to stay awake to keep him company until they got home.

The Hills had left Canada early in the afternoon, planning to stop and spend the night in a little motel along the way. But, talking and laughing together, they had lost all track of time. By 11:30, the little motels along the rural highway were all closed up tight.

Betty glanced at her husband, who was humming along with a song on the radio. "What time is it, honey?" she asked.

"Close to midnight," Barney replied. "This is a good time to travel. I haven't seen another car in half an hour."

The radio station they had been listening to suddenly faded out, and the soothing music was replaced by static. Barney clicked off the radio, and the two traveled in silence for a few moments.

Betty turned to look at the passing countryside, lit up by the huge full moon that hung in front of them, racing them home.

The field outside seemed extraordinarily bright. Betty glanced up at the sky and gasped.

"Stop! Pull over!" she cried. "Barney, pull over *now*!"

Puzzled, Barney pulled the car off the road and turned to his wife. She had grabbed the binoculars from the backseat and was gazing at something in the sky, something he couldn't see.

"What is it?" he asked. Betty said nothing. He touched her shoulder. She didn't move or speak.

Barney got out of the car and looked up in the direction his wife was staring. He let out a soft, low whistle.

Hovering in the sky above them was an aircraft unlike any Barney had ever seen before. An incredibly bright light radiated from the craft, bathing the nearby field in a beam of brilliant white. The craft was also making a buzzing, whirring noise. The beam of light seemed to pulsate and move in time with the rhythm of the noise.

"Amazing," Barney whispered. He moved to the passenger-side door and gently took the binoculars from his wife.

With the powerful binoculars in hand, Barney could

now study the strange craft carefully. It was beautiful, like some big, exotic bird that had appeared from nowhere. He could even make out two rows of windows. He trained the binoculars there, trying to see something inside the craft.

Then Barney's mouth went dry. He could see creatures moving around—and they were definitely not human.

Until that very moment, Barney Hill had thought he was looking at a brand-new, top-secret defense plane. Now he didn't know what the thing was. Panicky, he dropped the binoculars and raced around the back of the car. They had to get away!

But suddenly Barney stopped dead in his tracks. All thoughts of escape were replaced by one overwhelming desire. Barney Hill suddenly felt that he had to see the light up close, touch the light, be one with the light. He turned and started to walk toward the craft.

Inside the car, Betty Hill began to scream.

Chapter 2

John Loengard stared up at the chiseled features of Abraham Lincoln. He and Kimberly had made it. After months of planning and a long cross-country drive, they had arrived in the nation's capital.

President John F. Kennedy's inaugural speech had spurred Loengard to action. "Ask not what your country can do for you," the President had said. "Ask what you can do for your country." Loengard was in Washington to do his part. More than anything, he wanted to make a difference in the world.

Loengard looked at the wise face of Lincoln above him. "I'm here," he said softly, as much to himself as to the huge stone statue.

"Talk to yourself much?" asked a voice behind him.

Loengard turned to see his college sweetheart, Kimberly Sayers, smiling mischievously at him. She had been moved by Kennedy's speech, too. In fact, she had an interview for a part-time job at the White House—first thing the next morning.

"Just introducing myself to one of the most important people in Washington," Loengard replied.

"Let's go, John," Kimberly said. "You start work with Congressman Pratt tomorrow, and I've got a very important interview. Your conversation with Mr. Lincoln can wait."

Kimberly took Loengard's arm and led him down the steps, out of the shadows of the Lincoln Memorial and into the bright autumn sunshine. Loengard looked around and sighed happily. Everything was just perfect. The future seemed full of promise.

Little did he know that in less than three months, he would be plunged into a strange new world, one in which the future would be dark and unsettled. At the age of twenty-four, John Loengard thought he knew everything. He was about to find out that he knew nothing.

Loengard moved quickly and carefully through the tiny, cramped area that passed as Congressman Pratt's offices. He balanced a tray of coffee cups in one hand.

"Hello, Renee. One coffee, cream, no sugar." Loengard deposited a steaming cup on top of the secretary's desk next to a large stack of files. Renee, nodding her thanks, continued to deal with an irate caller at the other end of the phone line.

Loengard's official job title, Executive Assistant to the

Chief Aide, *sounded* good. It had impressed everyone back home. But the work itself was far less glamorous. In his first week on the job, Loengard's duties had included making copies, filing reports—and fetching coffee. He had come up with a new, more accurate job title for himself: Chief Gofer for All Office Employees. Loengard was far from discouraged, however. He knew that if he kept his eyes and ears open and worked hard, his chance to prove his worth would eventually come along.

Moving through the buzzing offices toward his own cluttered desk, Loengard heard the voice of his supervisor, Chief Aide Mark Simonson. Simonson was doing his best to explain an important bill to Congressman Pratt—no easy task.

"This is the *amendment* to the housing bill," said Simonson, speaking slowly and clearly, as if to a small child. "We are *against* the amendment and *for* the bill."

The congressman nodded vaguely, his mind obviously elsewhere.

Even though he'd been working for Congressman Pratt for only a short time, Loengard had quickly caught on that Simonson was the brains of the operation. Pratt just didn't seem to care about anything that slightly resembled politics.

Pratt's vague look suddenly disappeared. He grabbed a manila folder lying on the desk in front of him. "This was supposed to be delivered an hour ago," he said, waving the envelope in Simonson's face. "What is going on around here?"

"Congressman, I have to think that getting this amendment defeated is more important than delivering free tickets for the U.S. Mint tour," said the chief aide, frowning slightly.

Pratt, a tall, balding man with a dark, gloomy expression, moved closer to Simonson. "Son, think about this," he said. "Those people gave me a lot of money for my last campaign—a whole lot of money!"

Simonson's already flushed face turned a shade redder, and he opened his mouth to reply. Before he had a chance to say anything, Loengard swooped in to the rescue.

"Congressman, I can deliver that now," he said, taking the envelope from Pratt's hands. He turned to Simonson. "Mark, I'm sorry. I should have taken care of this yesterday like you asked."

Pratt looked carefully at the fresh-faced young man in the light brown suit who stood before him. "Loengard, you make sure those people know that I personally called in their favor." He grabbed his cup of coffee from the tray Loengard still carried and walked away.

"Thanks, John. I owe you one," Simonson said, sighing in relief. His face was just beginning to return to its normal color. "Sometimes I wonder how the Farmer keeps getting elected."

Simonson said he called Pratt "the Farmer" because the congressman was from a rural district in California. Loengard suspected the nickname had been inspired by Simonson's feeling that Pratt was better suited for farming than for politics.

"Just trying to help out," Loengard said. "You know, Mark, I could make things easier for you. You're overworked, and I'm bored."

"Look, I know you're being wasted. Welcome to Washington," Simonson said wearily.

"Come on, just give me a shot," pleaded Loengard. "I'll do anything."

He held his breath, waiting for Simonson's decision. When at long last Simonson nodded and said, "Follow me," Loengard exhaled sharply and smiled. He trailed his boss to a corner desk.

"The congressman has a budget subcommittee meeting at the end of the year. He wants to get rid of at least one of these programs." Simonson indicated a stack of files in the center of the desk. "Here's your job: Find out what each program is doing and what each one costs. Make each report three pages, typed, and don't use any big words. We want the Farmer to be able to understand them."

Loengard's eyes fixed eagerly on the files. He itched to pick them up and begin working. At last—an assignment he could sink his teeth into. Loengard knew that this job was his chance to shine. He would show Simonson how valuable he could be.

"Mark, you won't regret this," he said, tearing his eyes away from the files to look at Simonson. "Thank you."

Simonson smiled at his assistant. If he could bottle the kid's enthusiasm, he'd be a rich man. "Just don't forget that package," he said.

After Simonson left, Loengard picked up the folder on top of the stack. A typed label bearing the words *Project Blue Book* decorated the top left-hand corner of the file. A shiver of excitement ran down his spine. This was why he had come to Washington!

Loengard sat down at the desk, opened the file, and began to read. But after just a few sentences, he laughed and threw the folder down on the desk. Project Blue Book was an organization that investigated UFO sightings.

Chapter 3

Dayton, Ohio

John Loengard prided himself in being a very rational, intelligent person. He did not believe in ghosts, vampires, or werewolves. And he *definitely* did not believe in unidentified flying objects.

But at Wright-Patterson Air Force Base, he quickly realized that many people *did* believe in UFOs. Inside the small room that housed Project Blue Book, Loengard found filing cabinets stuffed full of reports from people around the nation—citizens who said they'd seen UFOs.

Loengard sat at a sturdy wooden table with twenty of the most recent reports spread out in front of him. He had already skimmed nearly ten of the files. Of the ten, Loengard thought that maybe two were worthy of further investigation. Just maybe.

"What do *you* make of all this stuff?" Loengard asked the Air Force lieutenant who had been assigned to keep an eye on him.

The lieutenant, seated at a nearby desk, said nothing. He continued to watch Loengard warily.

Loengard went back to his reading. As he pored over the records, he began to notice a pattern. Many witnesses reported seeing and hearing similar things: bright lights, strong winds, strange noises.

Descriptions from those who claimed to have seen the occupants of the crafts were also strikingly similar: huge heads that seemed too big for frail, sticklike bodies; large, almond-shaped eyes; gray, wrinkled skin.

Some witnesses reported losing time during the sightings. Some lost minutes. Others said they had lost days.

The door to the room creaked open, interrupting Loengard's thoughts. The lieutenant jumped to his feet and smartly saluted the uniformed officer who entered.

"Major Friend, sir," barked the lieutenant.

Loengard rose from his seat at the table and nodded at the tall, serious-looking man standing in the doorway. *Funny*, Loengard thought, *he doesn't look like the type who would believe in this nonsense.*

The officer approached the file-covered table and held out his hand. "You must be John Loengard," he said. "Major Robert Friend. I've been running Blue Book since 1958."

"Hello, Major," said Loengard. "Quite an impressive collection of reports you've gathered. They make for entertaining reading."

"Let's get right to the point, shall we?" said Friend. "Why has Pratt sent one of his eager beavers all the way from Washington to dig through our files?"

Loengard searched carefully for the correct words. How, exactly, do you tell a man that you're trying to put him out of business?

"Well," Loengard replied after a moment of awkward silence, "I think Congressman Pratt's just interested in making sure that the taxpayers get their money's worth."

Friend's eyes narrowed. "Really? Do you know how many cases we had last year?" he asked.

"Yes—557," said Loengard. He had done his homework.

"Very good," said Friend, nodding. "Now divide that number by three field investigators. Son, we're the biggest bargain around."

Loengard looked into the major's eyes. He took a deep breath and then spoke honestly. "Actually, I think Pratt is more concerned about whether we should be spending any money at all to investigate flying saucers," he said.

Friend did not seem surprised by the comment. "You're not a believer, I gather?" he asked.

For a split second, Loengard considered telling the major his view on UFOs: They were stories dreamed up by lonely or crazy people seeking attention. He decided against it.

"If I could, I'd like to continue looking through the most recent files you've got," Loengard said. "I'd like to narrow my search to the East Coast. My boss wants me to check out some of these 'witnesses' myself."

Friend turned to the lieutenant standing nearby. "Give him what he needs," the major said. "We've got nothing to hide."

"Thank you, Major," said Loengard. "Who knows? Maybe after I see what a bang-up job you're doing, I can convince the congressman that you need more funding."

Now it was Friend's turn to be skeptical. "I won't hold my breath," he replied.

Chapter 4

**December 1961
Portsmouth, New Hampshire**

Loengard drove slowly through the neat suburban neighborhood, scanning mailboxes and doors for number 31. He was looking for the home of Betty and Barney Hill, two of the last "witnesses" he would talk to before wrapping up his report on Project Blue Book. After weeks of talking to people who claimed to have seen UFOs, he remained unconvinced. According to Blue Book reports, many of the sightings were of low-flying planes or helicopters that had strayed from their flight paths. "Actual" UFO photos the agency had analyzed turned out to be fakes.

As Loengard had suspected, most of the people he interviewed were lonely, unstable, or looking for attention. The similarities in their stories could be explained. They all could have read the same story in a supermarket tabloid and run wild with it.

Even though he hadn't uncovered anything startling, Loengard's hard work had paid off at the office. Just a few days before this trip, Simonson had announced his promotion. His new job title was Congressional Investigator—even more impressive than the old title. Better still, he didn't have to fetch coffee for the staff anymore.

Loengard finally spotted a mailbox bearing the number 31. He parked his car at the curb, grabbed a large black case and a foil-wrapped plate from the seat next to him, and opened the door. The blast of cold winter air sent a chill through his body.

Loengard walked slowly, not only to avoid slipping on a patch of ice but also to get a good look at the Hills' home. It was a small but well-cared-for white Cape, much the same as the other houses on the block.

Loengard pressed the doorbell. He wondered if the other residents of Sycamore Street knew the Hills were probably as nutty as the fruitcake he was carrying.

A middle-aged woman answered the bell. *Looks too sensible to believe in flying saucers*, Loengard thought. Then again, Major Friend had also looked sensible.

"Can I help you?" the woman asked.

"Mrs. Hill? I'm John Loengard. I just drove over from Pease Air Force Base and—" Loengard was cut off in midsentence.

"Oh, please. I wish you people would just leave us alone. There's no use in talking about this anymore," said Betty Hill. She began to close the front door.

"Mrs. Hill, wait. I don't work for the Air Force. Remember, we talked on the phone? I'm from Congressman Charles Pratt's office," Loengard quickly explained. Holding out the foil-covered plate, he continued, "If you feel like talking, my girlfriend baked this fruitcake for us."

Betty seemed to relax a little. She opened the door wider. As she did, a tall man appeared behind her.

"Is there a problem here?" Barney Hill asked, putting his arm protectively around his wife.

"Oh, no, sir," Loengard responded. "I was just about to tell your wife that there's some new information about the sighting you reported."

"If all that is true, then why do you need a cake to talk your way in here?" Barney asked pointedly. He continued to regard Loengard with suspicion.

Most of the other witnesses had been dying to talk to Loengard, to tell their story one more time. The Hills were different. To hear what they had to say, Loengard realized, he was going to have to be straight-forward.

"You've got a good point there, sir. It was probably a pretty dumb idea," he admitted. "Look, I'll be honest with you. I was sent out to prove that the Air Force investigation is a waste of money. But right now, let's just say I've got an open mind."

Barney Hill hesitated a moment more. He and his wife exchanged a quick look. Betty nodded slightly.

"Come on in, then," he said finally, holding the door open.

"I'll get coffee," said Mrs. Hill, taking the fruitcake from Loengard. "Barney, make him comfortable in the living room."

Loengard followed Barney into a warm, cozy living room. A fire blazed in the fireplace. Two Christmas stockings hung nearby, and a brightly decorated Christmas tree stood in the corner.

Loengard set the black case on the floor next to the coffee table. "Do you mind if I tape what you have to say?" he asked.

"Go ahead," said Barney. "We've told our story many times, to many people—Air Force officials, police officers, reporters, you name it. If I thought I could find out what I saw, I would tell my story to the whole world."

By the time Loengard finished setting up his tape recorder, Mrs. Hill had returned with coffee and the fruitcake, sliced into small, equal pieces.

Loengard waited until the Hills were settled on the sofa in front of the fireplace. Then he flipped the switch to start the tape machine. He sat near the fire, enjoying the heat and the warm glow of the flames.

"Whenever you're ready," he said.

For a few moments, neither Betty nor Barney Hill said a word. Mrs. Hill gazed out the window. Mr. Hill looked down at his hands. Finally he began.

"We were returning from a vacation in Canada, driving down Route Three through the White Mountains to Portsmouth," he said.

As the Hills talked, Loengard found himself being drawn in. The two were obviously telling what they thought to be the truth. They were earnest and believable.

The night that had changed the Hills' lives was about to change John Loengard's. If he had known what was about to happen, he might have gotten up and run out of the house. Instead, he stayed and began to believe.

John Loengard's descent into a strange, dark world had begun.

Two blocks away, a delivery van painted with a logo for Mother May's Home-Style Breads was parked in front of a vacant house. The cargo wasn't fresh bread, however. The van held sophisticated wiretapping equipment.

In the back of the van, two men dressed in delivery uniforms listened intently through the headsets they wore. The two men were "cloakers," agents of the top-secret organization known only as Majestic.

The cloakers were listening to the Hills tell John Loengard about their experience last year. Majestic had planted bugs—small hidden microphones—throughout the Hills' house.

"Were you captured by the creatures?" Loengard asked the Hills.

"We're not sure what happened," said Barney Hill. "One minute we were looking at the craft. Next thing we know, we're back in our car. But it's *two hours later*!"

The two men inside the van looked at each other. After weeks of snooping, Loengard was starting to believe that these people had really seen something. If he took his beliefs back to Pratt, the cloakers knew he could cause serious trouble.

The congressman might draw public attention to Project Blue Book. And that, the cloakers knew, would be a disaster. They continued to listen carefully.

"Wait till the congressman hears this. I don't see how he can ignore your story," Loengard said. "I wouldn't be surprised if he asked you to testify before Congress about this matter."

Immediately the cloaker known as Steele ripped off his headset, picked up a telephone, and dialed. Waiting for an answer, he unconsciously touched the gun hidden under his delivery jacket.

For weeks, Steele had trailed Loengard as he inched

toward the truth. Although Steele's boss, the captain, didn't think the snooping aide was a threat, Steele had known better. He'd had a bad feeling about Loengard.

Now the captain will have to take care of this nosy little pest, Steele thought. *And I'll be there for the fireworks.*

Chapter 5

Loengard sped down the dark country road on his way home to Washington. His head was spinning with the tale the Hills had told him. The story sounded crazy, but crazier still was the fact that Loengard absolutely believed the couple.

He turned on the radio for company, but he barely heard the music blaring through the speakers. His hands gripped the steering wheel tightly as bits of the conversation replayed over and over in his head.

Loengard's thoughts snapped quickly back to the present as the car filled with the loud, crackling sound of static. He leaned forward and fiddled with the radio dial. Nothing but static. He shut the radio off.

Glancing in his rearview mirror, Loengard froze. A strong, bright light flashed in the mirror, then was gone. Loengard quickly craned his neck around to peer out the rear window. Nothing.

The Hills' story really spooked me, Loengard thought, trying to be rational and laugh off the uneasy feeling creeping steadily into the pit of his stomach.

He turned to look at the road again, and there it was, dead ahead. It was just as the Hills had described it: a strange black craft hovering in the sky.

The sick feeling in Loengard's stomach turned to terror as a beam of light burst from the thing, piercing the darkness. The light searched for and found its target—Loengard's car.

Loengard turned the steering wheel sharply to the right. The car veered off the road, came to rest in a ditch, and stalled. Panicked, he turned the key in the ignition. "Please start, please start, please start," he said over and over. But the car was dead. In his desperation to escape the mysterious craft, he had flooded the engine with gas.

Loengard pushed his door open. If the Hills' story was true, then the aliens had taken Betty Hill right out of her car. He preferred to give the creatures a run for their money.

Loengard spotted a grove of trees about two hundred yards away. Could he make it? He didn't know, but he was going to try. As he ran, the light from the spacecraft above tracked his every move.

He tried to concentrate on the trees, but bits of the conversation with the Hills popped maddeningly into his mind.

Static on the radio . . . strange, piercing light . . . loud whirring noise. He had no doubt that the thing chasing him was the same thing the Hills had seen.

Just as Loengard thought he was home free, the black shape dropped from the sky and landed directly in front of him. The bright light shone into his eyes, blinding him.

Frozen by fear, Loengard watched in horror as four dark shapes exited the craft. The sight spurred him into action, and he turned to run. The shapes were quick, however, and Loengard was knocked roughly to the ground.

Rolling over onto his back, Loengard saw the "aliens" for what they were: four human men wearing thick winter coats over their dark suits.

The spacecraft, Loengard saw, was a large black helicopter. Although he should have been comforted by the sight of the helicopter, he was still terrified. The chopper had been after him!

Three of the men stepped back to allow the fourth to approach Loengard. The man had an air of strength and authority that surrounded him like a cloak. He held out his hand and pulled Loengard easily to his feet. Two of the men immediately grabbed him and held him firmly.

"Very impressive, Mr. Loengard," said the man. "You've got real talent."

"Who are you?" Loengard asked. "How do you know my name?"

The man didn't bother to answer Loengard's questions. Without taking his eyes off the frightened young investigator for a second, he nodded toward Loengard's car.

"Get his tape," the man commanded.

"Yes, Captain." One of the other men standing nearby scurried away.

"Let me set the record straight for you, John," said the captain. "Betty and Barney Hill saw an airplane go off course. They're not going to testify before Congress, Pratt, or anybody else. Is that clear?"

The man's voice was icily arrogant. Loengard wondered whether anyone had ever disobeyed the captain. All he knew for sure was that he didn't want to be the first. He tried to speak, but words wouldn't come. He could only nod his agreement.

"Good," the captain said. A ghost of a smile flickered across his face—there and gone in seconds. He turned to leave.

Loengard found his voice. "Who are you?" he asked. He knew he must sound terrified. That was okay. He *was* terrified.

The captain wheeled around. He strode toward Loengard, stopping just inches away. Loengard could feel the man's breath on his face.

"I am just a figment of your imagination. I do not exist," the captain whispered menacingly. "This incident never happened. Tomorrow you will file a report with Pratt telling him Project Blue Book doesn't cost enough money to merit his attention. In other words, John, leave Blue Book alone."

The final sentence was part statement, part threat. Loengard trembled.

The captain seemed about to say more when the second man returned with Loengard's tape.

"Got it," the man said, holding out the recording of the Hills' story.

The captain pocketed the tape, then looked at the thin-faced man who had retrieved it. Loengard looked, too, and shivered. The captain was frightening, but Thin-Face looked absolutely dangerous. And at that moment, his unwanted attention was directed at Loengard.

Thin-Face moved closer. He opened his coat and withdrew a gun from his holster. He pointed the gun directly at Loengard.

"You want me to put him to bed?" Thin-Face asked the captain.

The captain nodded, then turned on his heel and walked toward the waiting helicopter.

"Wait, please, I haven't done anything!" Loengard screamed after the retreating captain. "No, no, nooo—"

His cries were cut off by a loud click as the man pulled the trigger. The gun was empty!

Loengard's legs buckled and he nearly fell over. Only the captain's two flunkies kept him upright.

Thin-Face leaned over Loengard as he gasped for air. "You're lucky, college boy; the man says you get to stay up late. Keep your nose out of our business. Or next time, we'll make a house call."

Thin-Face shoved Loengard roughly, sending him sprawling to the ground. Then, as suddenly as they had appeared, the men disappeared. Loengard vaguely heard the sound of the helicopter as it lifted off and flew overhead.

For what seemed like hours, Loengard lay on the ground, shaking and trembling. Finally, he picked himself up and headed back to his car.

The next day, Loengard stood in front of the Capitol, rubbing his hands together for warmth against the cold, gray day. He was already late for work, but he couldn't bring himself to go inside. Last night's events were still fresh in his mind. He had been unable to sleep a wink, and each time he thought of what had happened he began to shake again.

Suddenly Loengard heard the buzz of a helicopter, and his eyes darted toward the sky. False alarm. Just a normal chopper. He wondered if he would ever see things the same way again. Everything now looked dark, dismal, and dangerous.

Loengard finally forced himself inside and trudged up the stairs toward Pratt's offices. On his desk, he found a three-page, typewritten report labeled *Project Blue Book*. How had they gotten this in here?

He flipped quickly through the report. They hadn't missed anything—they'd even managed to forge his signature on the last page.

Loengard was suddenly angry. How dare these people? They might have scared him witless last night, but they would need to do a lot more to make John Loengard jump through their hoops.

He began to throw the report into the trash can, then froze as he felt a heavy hand slap his shoulder. Turning, he saw the friendly face of Mark Simonson.

"Hey, John, you're a little jumpy," Simonson said. "What's this?" He grabbed the report on Blue Book from Loengard's hands.

Loengard tried to take back the report, but Simonson had already begun reading.

"Project Blue Book," he said. "Don't you sleep? I was going to give you till the end of the week to finish this."

Simonson thumbed through the report until he reached the section titled *Summary*. "'In summary, Project Blue

Book is a useful organization,'" Simonson read directly
from the report. "'A detailed cost analysis shows that
cutting Blue Book would have little effect on the budget.'
Well, well, Loengard. Pretty bold for your first memo."

"You don't understand, Mark. I didn't write this,"
Loengard said. "Please, I need your help."

Simonson looked closely at Loengard. The usually
confident and self-assured young man looked like he'd
had the wind knocked out of him. "Come on, we'll talk in
my office." Simonson motioned for Loengard to follow
him.

Inside, Loengard told Simonson what had happened,
beginning with the Hills' story and ending with the evil-
looking man's deadly warning. He talked quickly, feeling
the weight of the story lift from him.

When Loengard finished, he glanced up at Simonson.
Seeing the expression on his boss's face, he felt better.
The story had seemed almost unreal this morning, even
to him. He was gratified that Simonson believed him.

"Helicopter, wiretaps. Do you have any idea what
you've stumbled onto, John?" Simonson asked. He
rubbed his chin thoughtfully.

"The Hills definitely saw something," Loengard said.
"What it was, I don't know."

"Probably some secret weapon we're going to surprise
the Russians with," Simonson said.

"In New Hampshire?" Loengard asked.

"Oh, I don't know, a test flight, maybe," Simonson responded. "But I think you've discovered something really big. Maybe somebody's using federal dollars illegally. Who knows? Whatever they're doing, you've caught them red-handed."

"I didn't catch anybody," Loengard reminded him. "They caught me. And I think these guys are dangerous, Mark. They really scared me."

"So consider this your chance to get even," Simonson said, smiling.

Suddenly Pratt poked his head in. "Simonson, what's going on?" he asked gruffly. "Or is my ten o'clock briefing at ten-thirty these days?"

"Sorry, Congressman, I was just going over Loengard's trip," Simonson replied. He kept the report hidden behind his back.

Pratt turned to Loengard. "So is this Blue Book worth its salt?" he asked. For once, he seemed genuinely interested in Loengard's reply.

"I'm working on the report now, sir," Loengard said. Pratt grunted and disappeared.

Simonson turned excitedly to Loengard. "We'll keep quiet about this until you can dig up more information. John, this could be our big chance. We could score some major points here. Who knows what could come of this?"

Loengard considered his eager boss. His own thoughts were less enthusiastic. Of course Mark was excited. He wasn't the one who'd been run off the road and had a gun pointed at his head.

"Don't worry, I'll cover for you with Pratt," Simonson said, misreading Loengard's discouraged expression. "Just consider this some extra-credit work."

Loengard rose from his seat and started for the door.

"And John—keep your head down," Simonson said.

Chapter 6

Loengard lay on the sofa in his small apartment, a cup of coffee in his hands. Over the past weeks, he had worked feverishly to unwrap the mystery he'd stumbled upon.

He'd spent days in the Library of Congress, reading everything he could find about flying saucers. He'd read old newspapers dating back to the 1940s, looking for articles about UFO sightings. He had also become fiercely determined to track down the man who had terrorized him in December. All he'd had to work with was the man's title—Captain.

Loengard began his hunt for the captain by looking through old Navy personnel files. Slowly Loengard's research led him to a man whose promising career in the Navy had taken a strange twist after World War II: Captain Frank Bach, U.S. Navy.

Many times during the past weeks, Loengard had felt like quitting. He was glad now that he had stuck it out. After Loengard told Simonson of his new knowledge,

Simonson decided that the two of them would confront Bach—once they learned where he was. Loengard sipped his coffee and considered the best way of finding the captain.

His thoughts on the subject were interrupted by the ringing telephone. Picking up the receiver, he heard his boss's familiar voice. Simonson sounded upset. "John, turn on your TV. Channel six," he said.

Loengard stretched forward and flipped on the television. There on the screen stood none other than Captain Frank Bach. He was guiding another man into a waiting car. Soldiers and official-looking men watched the event.

"The pictures that you're seeing show Lieutenant Francis Gary Powers, the American U-2 pilot shot down over the Soviet Union in 1960," the newscaster said. "After being held by the Soviets for nearly two years, Powers is finally being freed. He is being exchanged for Soviet spy Colonel Rudolph Abel."

"That's your Captain Bach, isn't it?" Simonson asked, already knowing the answer. "Listen, if Bach was sent to pick up Powers, then he's more important and powerful than we thought."

"Maybe Powers is involved with this," Loengard said excitedly. "Mark, we've got to talk to him."

"Forget it," Simonson said. "If Powers is involved,

then the *President* must be in on it, too. Who do you think arranged Powers's release? John, this isn't some military budget scandal anymore. This is quicksand."

"But, Mark, this is the break we've been waiting for," Loengard said.

"Not me," said Simonson. "I've got a wife and kids. I'm out. It's over, you hear me? Over."

After Simonson hung up, Loengard turned his attention back to the newscast.

"Later this morning, Powers will address a closed-door session of the Senate Armed Services Committee. In other news . . ."

Loengard clicked off the TV and raced into the bedroom. He now knew how to get to Captain Bach. And he didn't want to be late.

Loengard stood anxiously in the Senate Office Building, eyeing a nearby door. The sign posted in front of the door read *Senate Armed Services Committee— Closed Session.*

In about twenty minutes, Francis Gary Powers would be in that room, giving his testimony. Now it was just a question of when Powers would show up—and with whom.

Loengard didn't have to wait long to find out. Moments later, an elevator door slid open and Powers, still escorted by Bach, stepped out. Loengard moved forward, but the two were immediately surrounded by TV cameras and reporters shouting questions.

Disappointed, Loengard stepped back. Seeing Bach again sent a familiar thrill of fear through his body. But Loengard's desire to know what Bach was involved with was even stronger. He watched as Bach propelled Powers toward the door. After Powers was inside, Bach turned and pushed his way back through the reporters. He found a bench near the elevator doors, sat down, and lit up a cigarette. Loengard took a deep breath and stepped forward.

"A new report from the surgeon general says those things can kill you," he said, sitting next to Bach.

Bach glanced at Loengard. If the captain was surprised to see him there, he didn't show it.

"All our days are numbered," Bach answered. He turned and looked directly into Loengard's eyes. "Some people's more than others."

"I'm a member of the congressional staff. You can't rough me up here." Loengard tried hard to sound cool and in control. His insides felt like ice water. The sound of a clicking gun flashed briefly through his head.

"How's your 'extra-credit work' coming, John?" Bach asked pointedly.

"Not bad, *Captain Bach*," Loengard replied. "I don't

exactly know whom you work for now, but I'm pretty close to the truth."

Bach didn't seem interested. "The truth is overrated," he said.

"Maybe," Loengard replied. "But what you're doing can't stay hidden forever." Loengard moved his coat aside to give Bach a glimpse of the piece of paper resting in his suit pocket. "I've got a subpoena here from the U.S. Congress. You *have* to talk to me. If you cooperate fully, I will protect our conversations. You will not be named as a source in any hearing or investigation."

Bach was not impressed. Stubbing out his cigarette, he rose and pressed the elevator button. Loengard followed, determined to get some answers. "I've read about Roswell. I know about Project Sign and Project Grudge," he told Bach. "I already know a lot more than you think I do."

That seemed to get Bach's attention. He turned to Loengard and looked at him carefully. "What else do you *think* you know?" Bach asked.

"Flying saucers don't come from outer space," Loengard said. "You're building them, aren't you?"

Bach stepped closer to Loengard. He reached into the young man's coat and pulled out the "subpoena." It was Loengard's laundry receipt. Bach threw the paper to the ground. "You're pretty brave, aren't you, son?" he said.

"When I have to be," Loengard replied.

The elevator doors slid open, and Bach stepped in. "You have to understand, Mr. Loengard," he said. "The truth has a price. You have to decide whether you're willing to pay it."

Loengard hesitated. The truth was within his reach, just beyond the elevator doors. What else was waiting for him there?

He stepped quickly into the elevator.

Chapter 7

The Outskirts of Washington, D.C.

Loengard tried to question Bach as they drove, but the man was silent. Eventually Loengard gave up and looked out the window. He wondered where their ride would end.

After driving for miles through the woods, Loengard realized that he had absolutely no idea where they were. He would never be able to find his way back. He was completely at Bach's mercy.

They finally pulled up to a huge security gate. Reaching below his seat, Bach grabbed a small device and pressed a button on it. The security gate swung open, and Bach drove inside. Looking out the back window, Loengard saw the gate automatically close again behind them.

Loengard soon saw their destination: a seemingly ordinary cement building. Bach pulled into the reserved parking space closest to the entrance. A sign in front of the space said *MJ-1*. Whatever was going on inside the building, Bach was in charge of it.

Loengard followed the captain to the entrance. Bach punched a code on a number pad near the side of the door. The door slid open, and Bach entered. Loengard hesitated.

"You've already decided to go through this door," Bach said without turning. "Don't act like you have to think about it."

Loengard followed Bach through a maze of corridors. "Where are we?" he asked. Again, no answer was forthcoming.

The place was much larger than it looked from the outside. It seemed to Loengard that they were heading downward, but he couldn't be certain. He felt totally disoriented.

The two came at last to a checkpoint before a set of double doors. Two heavily armed guards saluted Bach.

"Take your coat off," Bach instructed Loengard. Then, to a guard, "Search him. Log him in."

The guard patted Loengard down thoroughly, then clipped an ID badge on him. Loengard looked at the badge uneasily. It already had his picture on it.

Loengard watched as the other guard held his arm out to Captain Bach. The guard had a large briefcase attached to his wrist by a metal handcuff. Bach unlocked the cuffs and took the case.

Bach led Loengard through the double doors. Inside,

at least fourteen people, most of them wearing military uniforms, sat in front of computers and flashing control panels. The room hummed with activity.

"This is Majestic Twelve, the highest-level security organization you've never heard of," said Bach. "This is our control room. All our information comes in through here. It's Majestic's nerve center."

Bach guided Loengard through the room and out into another wide corridor. "Get in," he said, gesturing at the small electric car waiting there.

"Where are you taking me?" Loengard asked, climbing into the car.

"You said you wanted the truth," Bach responded, starting the car. "The truth is down this hallway, third door on the right."

As they sped down the long corridor, Loengard could feel his excitement building. When the car stopped, he jumped out, itching to be inside. He waited impatiently for Bach to open the door.

Once inside, though, he couldn't hide his disappointment. The room held nothing but a stainless steel operating table. Two rows of stainless steel drawers, one on top of the other, were built into the far wall.

"When I was your age, I had my sights set on becoming an admiral," Bach said from behind him, closing and locking the door. "But a top-secret Navy incident landed me in Roswell, at our only nuclear bomber base."

Loengard turned to face Bach. "So those stories about the UFO crash-landing in Roswell, they're all true?" he asked.

"Nothing is *all* true," Bach replied. "It depends whom you ask. If you had asked Mac Brazel what crashed on his farm on July 3, 1947, he probably would have told you it was one of these."

Bach pulled a photo from the briefcase and gave it to Loengard. The photo showed a disk-shaped saucer that had crashed in the middle of a field.

"The news reported that he had changed his mind," Loengard said as he studied the picture. "He thought it was really a weather balloon."

"What the news reports doesn't always matter," said Bach.

Loengard handed the photo back to Bach. "Blue Book doesn't have anything like this," he said.

"We gather all physical evidence before they get to it," Bach replied.

"So what you're saying is that Project Blue Book is just a front for Majestic?" Loengard asked.

Bach nodded. He reached into his shirt and pulled out a rectangular silver box no more than three inches long and two inches wide. The box hung on a chain around his neck. He removed the box from its chain and held it out to Loengard.

"Open it up. Take a look," he said.

Loengard took the box from Bach and slowly slid the top open. Lying in the box was a tiny triangular object. It looked like it was made of waxed paper.

"Take it out," Bach urged him.

Loengard held the box upside down over his palm and gave it a shake. The object dropped onto his hand. It rapidly unfolded, forming another triangle three times its original size. Strange designs covered the shape.

Surprised, Loengard let go of the triangle, expecting it to drop to the floor. To his amazement, it hovered in the air in front of him, moving slightly, as if it were swaying in a light breeze.

Loengard reached out and cautiously touched the triangle. It began to spin rapidly, whirling dizzily in midair. The thing was amazing! But what exactly was it? Loengard turned and looked questioningly at Bach.

Bach leaned over and grabbed an edge of the spinning object. It folded back into itself until it was once more just a tiny, ordinary-looking triangle. Bach pushed the shape back into the silver box and closed the lid.

"It's from the Roswell crash," he said. "I wear this so I'll remember that whoever builds these things has knowledge far greater than our own."

"Do you think it's the Russians?" Loengard asked. He immediately regretted his question. Bach was looking at him as if he was stupid or unimaginative—or both.

Bach turned his back on Loengard and strode across the room to the wall of drawers. He began to rapidly spin a combination lock on one drawer. When the lock clicked, Bach pulled it open.

Only then did Loengard understand what the drawers were for. *Oh, no,* he thought, *this is a morgue!*

Inside the drawer, a body of some sort was covered with a thick plastic sheet. Loengard could make out the shadowy outline of a head, but that was all. He stepped closer.

"You tell me," Bach said, watching Loengard approach. "Does this look Russian to you?" With that, he pulled the plastic sheet off the body.

Loengard gasped. There, in the drawer, lay the body of a creature that could not possibly be human. Its large, round head looked far too big for the rest of its body. Huge, almond-shaped eyes stared sightlessly up at Loengard. The thing looked as if it had been dead for some time—its gray skin was wrinkled like the skin of a mummy. It lay forever frozen in a fetal position, its tiny mouth open as if it had uttered one final scream before dying.

From the countless hours of research and interviewing

he had done, Loengard knew what the creature was. He could no longer deny the truth—this thing was from outer space.

A wave of nausea ran over Loengard, and he stumbled backward, wanting to get as far from the body as possible. Feeling his legs about to give way, he sank to his knees and covered his face with his hands. The image of the shriveled thing in the drawer refused to go away.

"We call it a *Gray*," Bach explained. He closed the door and gave the lock a spin. Then he crossed the room and helped Loengard to his feet. "Don't be embarrassed, John. Most people have trouble digesting the truth," he said.

Bach waited until Loengard had regained some control. Then he said, "Here's the way it works. No one who joins Majestic can talk about this to anyone outside. It's a very exclusive club."

"Wait a minute," Loengard protested. "I haven't joined anything."

"Every day you pursued us was another knock at the door," Bach replied. He pulled a file labeled *John Loengard* from the briefcase and handed it to Loengard.

Loengard opened the file. Inside was a series of photos. In one, he was at the Library of Congress, researching UFOs. In another, he was at the home of a Navy admiral's widow, looking through the dead man's top-secret files. Photo after photo showed him at every stage of his investigation.

With a sinking feeling, Loengard realized that while he had been tracking Bach, he himself had been tracked! *I never even suspected,* he thought bitterly.

"You recruited yourself," Bach said when Loengard closed the file. "I'm giving you the chance to serve your country in a way few people ever have."

"What if I say no?" Loengard asked, already knowing what Bach's answer would be.

"You can't," Bach said.

Loengard got out of his car and walked up the stairs to his apartment. He had accomplished his goal. He had found Bach, and he had learned the truth. But with his newfound knowledge came many new questions. Did he want the answers?

Loengard glanced left and right, wondering whether someone was watching, photographing his every move. Inside his apartment, he moved swiftly from room to room, drawing the curtains tight. When the phone rang, he actually jumped. He picked up the receiver and waited.

"John, I met her!" Kimberly's voice bubbled over the line. "I met Jackie Kennedy! I've been hired to work on this TV special she's doing. It's only temporary, but isn't that the most exciting thing you've ever heard? I'll be in the White House!"

"Congratulations, Kim. You deserve it," Loengard said, forcing some enthusiasm into his voice. Kimberly was intelligent, easygoing, and personable. Everyone she met liked her immediately. Loengard knew that Kimberly was at the start of a bright future. He also knew he needed to protect her from the darkness that was consuming him.

"I'll come over and we can celebrate," Kim said. "But first, tell me about *your* day."

Loengard took a deep breath. "Oh, you know. Nothing special," he said.

Chapter 8

March 1962

For two short weeks, John Loengard's life continued much as it had before he joined Majestic. Bach had made it clear that Loengard was to keep his job with Congressman Pratt. So each morning, Loengard awoke and went into the office and did his work, trying to act as normal as possible. He was quite good at living the lie—nobody seemed to notice that he was a changed person.

Bach had also made it clear that when Majestic called, Loengard must be ready to answer. So Loengard was not surprised to see a Majestic agent waiting for him one morning outside his apartment. Loengard looked at the man with dislike: He was the agent who had pointed the gun at him in December.

"Well, well, it's the college boy," the agent said sarcastically. "Got your diploma right here."

He handed Loengard a plane ticket, then started to walk briskly away.

"Wait a minute," Loengard shouted after him. "This

is a one-way ticket. When am I coming back? What am I doing? What's the job?"

His questions were useless. The Majestic agent disappeared into a waiting car. Loengard went back inside to pack.

Loengard was met at a small airport in Boise, Idaho, by the same agent, whose name turned out to be Steele. Steele led him to a waiting helicopter. Bach and two other Majestic agents were already on board.

Once the chopper was in the air, Loengard tried his best to make small talk with the agents riding in the back. The men eyed him suspiciously and said nothing.

"Outside! Nine o'clock!" Bach called from the cockpit.

Loengard helped an agent open the helicopter's door. Staring at the ground below, he didn't need to ask what he was looking for. There, in a large wheat field, he could see a huge pattern of some sort.

"It looks like a diagram or maybe a map symbol," Loengard said.

One wheat field had been marked with a large triangle that had a circle inside it. A straight line from the top of the triangle stretched across a dirt road and into another field, connecting to a small circle that had four lines inside it.

"Why would anybody smart enough to make one of those be so dumb as to put it out there for the whole world to see?" asked an agent.

"They didn't, Popejoy," Bach responded. "We're thirty miles from nowhere. Last week a private pilot who got lost reported this to the local sheriff's office."

"Why didn't the farmer who owns the field report it?" Loengard asked.

"Good question," said Bach. "All we've got is his name. Grantham. Elliot P. Grantham."

Steele's eyes shone. "Are we going to roll him at his house or take him on a field trip?" he asked.

"Neither. John here is going to pay him a visit and sweet-talk some answers out of him," said Bach.

Steele snickered and rolled his eyes.

Two hours later, Loengard found himself driving toward the home of farmer Elliot P. Grantham. He wore a microphone securely taped to his body. On his coat, he sported a small plastic badge that identified him as Fred Grabar, County Extension Agent.

"That's you," Popejoy had said, pinning the badge on him. "Don't sweat it. Boss wouldn't have picked you unless he thought you could do it."

As he drove up Grantham's driveway, Loengard recalled the instructions Bach had given him.

"You're here to ask questions," Bach had said. "Whoever made the markings in that field is probably long gone by now. We need a solid witness." Then, almost as an afterthought, he'd added, "We'll be nearby in case anything gets hairy."

What exactly does Bach expect to happen here? Loengard wondered as he pulled up in front of a red barn and got out. Given the way the place looked, he didn't think he'd have any trouble with Grantham.

The farm was like something from the cover of the *Saturday Evening Post.* A few chickens scratched in front of a tired old farmhouse. On the big front porch, a swing swayed gently in the mild breeze. The weather vane on the roof creaked, turning slowly.

Loengard heard the tinny sound of a transistor radio coming from inside the barn. He stepped into the shadows of the old building, pausing for a moment to allow his eyes to adjust to the darkness.

"Mr. Grantham?" he called. No answer. Loengard stepped deeper into the barn, trying to locate the radio.

"Who wants to know?" boomed a voice behind him.

Loengard whirled around, coming face-to-face with a white-haired man dressed in overalls. The man held a long screwdriver and waved it at Loengard like a sword.

"My name's Fred Grabar," said Loengard, surprised at

how easily the lie slipped off his tongue. "I'm from the County Extension Service."

"I didn't call you," Grantham said. He looked Loengard up and down suspiciously.

"My office got a call about some kind of strange formation in your field. They sent me out here to investigate it."

Grantham turned away. "I ain't talking about it," he said.

"Well, sir, you might want to change your mind about that," said Loengard, thinking fast. "You see, the law says if you've had crops ruined as a result of vandalism, and I have to assume that this *is* vandalism, then you qualify for government funds."

Grantham seemed more interested now. "You mean you'd pay me money?" he asked.

"That's right," Loengard said.

Grantham thought for a moment. "All right. We'll take my truck. Field's too far for walking."

The old farmer didn't say a word during the mile-long drive out to the field. He stopped his truck where the strange marking crossed from one field to the next over the dirt road.

Loengard got out of the truck and stooped down. He picked up a handful of the white, chalklike substance that made up the marking.

Loengard followed the line off the road and into the field that contained the triangular shape. He came to the place where a barbed-wire fence had once stood. Where the marking crossed the fencing, the barbed wire had completely disappeared. Loengard reached out and touched the end of the remaining fence. It flaked away like ash. Whatever had made the marking had burned right through the wire!

Loengard continued farther into the field. From the sky, the marking had looked big. Only now, however, did he get a true sense of how huge the thing actually was.

"Do you remember the first time you saw this?" he shouted back at Grantham, who had remained inside the truck.

"Last week, maybe," Grantham replied. "I don't come down here much this time of year."

"Why didn't you report it?" Loengard asked.

"Ain't no law says I got to," Grantham said.

"You see any strange lights in the sky over the last month or two?" Loengard asked.

Grantham raised his eyebrows. "Why? You seen some?" he said.

Loengard ignored the sarcasm in Grantham's voice and went back to work. He bent down to examine the formation more closely. "This is incredible," he whispered into the hidden microphone. "The stalks are laid down perfectly. It looks like they're woven together."

He straightened up and walked a bit farther. Suddenly he felt something beneath his feet—something solid and unyielding.

"I've found something," Loengard said softly. He reached down and pulled the wheat away, revealing a small metal triangle. Etched in the triangle was the pattern that had been laid out in the field. Loengard picked the triangle up to inspect it more closely.

"Whatever it is, it looks like it's made of gold," he said for the benefit of Bach and the others. "It's that design again—the one on the triangle you showed me, Captain."

Loengard ran his fingers over the symbol. Who could have put the thing here? And why? He'd seen what Bach's strange little triangle could do. What might this one be capable of?

Loengard considered the possibilities: Perhaps the symbol was a compass of some sort, marking the field as an alien landing strip or an information center. The metal triangle might be some kind of receiver, placed here to send signals back to alien spacecraft. *But who would send those signals?* Loengard wondered.

His thoughts were interrupted by the sound of a revving engine. Loengard looked up to see Grantham's truck barreling toward him. The farmer was trying to run him down!

Loengard dropped the triangle and dived headfirst into the wheat field.

"Help! He's trying to kill me!" he screamed, hoping for the first time that Bach and the others were close by.

Loengard quickly assessed the situation. Should he stay down and hope that Grantham would be unable to find him? Looking around, he realized that wouldn't work. The weight of his body had flattened the wheat stalks. Grantham would be able to track him easily. Loengard would have to dodge the old man until Bach arrived.

Loengard jumped to his feet and began running toward the dirt road. From behind, he heard the loud snarling of the truck. He turned quickly and saw that Grantham was closing in fast. Loengard waited until the very last second, then dived again into the wheat field.

The old farmer hit the brakes and turned for another shot at Loengard. Then, thankfully, Bach and the others were there, tearing into the field in a dark sedan. Popejoy and Steele were already leaning out the windows, guns in hand.

Loengard watched as the sedan took off in hot pursuit of Grantham. The farmer's old truck was no match for the newer, faster car. The Majestic agents soon closed the gap between the two vehicles, and shots rang out across the field.

One bullet found its mark, puncturing the truck's left front tire. The vehicle began to weave dizzily. Grantham struggled to keep his truck under control, but he veered suddenly into a steep culvert. Loengard watched in horror as the truck rolled over twice before coming to rest on its wheels.

By the time Loengard reached Popejoy, standing outside the car, Bach and Steele were returning from the truck.

"Grantham's dead," Bach said. "We're taking his body to Majestic. Steele, get some people out here to photograph the scene. Then get rid of that formation in the field."

Loengard looked toward the truck, shaken. He had never been this close to death before. He leaned heavily against the car, trying to sort out what had just happened. Why had Grantham tried to murder him?

Steele glanced at Loengard's pale face. "Get used to it, college boy," he said. "The ride's just starting."

Chapter 9

Majestic

Loengard watched as Majestic's two head scientists, Dr. Hertzog and Dr. Halligan, examined Grantham's remains. Halligan held what looked like a medical report.

"According to his family physician, your man rarely smoked or drank. No history of cancer, no surgeries, and no long stays in the hospital," Halligan read.

"Just an ordinary man," Hertzog commented.

"Ordinary men do not try to run down complete strangers with their pickup trucks," said Bach.

"Well, let's remove the cranial cap first," said Hertzog. "Perhaps he had a brain tumor that affected his behavior." He turned on a small electric saw and leaned over the body.

As the doctor brought the saw closer to Grantham's body, the dead man's face twitched, as if in fear of the instrument.

"What the . . . ?" the doctor shouted. "He moved!" His saw clattered to the floor as he stumbled back from the table.

Bach and Steele stepped in close to inspect the corpse.

Loengard decided to stay put. "Could it be one of those involuntary responses dead bodies sometimes make?" he asked from across the room. He hoped the doctor would have an easy medical explanation for this.

"Not likely," Halligan replied.

"Doctor, is this man dead or not?" Bach asked.

Recovering his nerve, Hertzog stepped forward. "There is no heartbeat. No pupil dilation, either," he said, checking Grantham for vital signs. Hertzog began to pry open the dead man's mouth with a tongue depressor. Almost immediately, Grantham's teeth clenched shut, snapping the wooden implement in half.

Bach turned to Popejoy. "We are now officially Red-Ultra. Secure the entire sector. Go to cold storage. Bring back specimen A-three." Bach spat out the commands like bullets. "And Popejoy, lock this door—from the outside."

"What exactly is going on here?" Hertzog demanded nervously. "We need to know what you're up to."

"Something is inside that man's head, and I want it taken out without damage," Bach replied.

"Damage to whom?" Hertzog shouted at the captain. "For Pete's sake, Bach—"

Grantham's right hand shot up from the table and

seized Hertzog's throat. The doctor's eyes widened, and his face turned an alarming shade of red as he gasped for air.

Loengard instinctively jumped forward and grabbed Grantham's arm. He tried to pry the hand from around Hertzog's throat. The dead farmer's grip was like iron.

"Help me!" he yelled to the others in the room.

Steele came to his aid. Together, the two men were able to free Hertzog from Grantham's deadly grasp. The doctor fell to the floor, clutching his neck and sucking huge gulps of air into his aching lungs.

"Hold the body down," Bach commanded his two agents. He turned to Halligan. "Get me a container with a lid."

As Loengard and Steele grabbed Grantham, the corpse suddenly stopped convulsing and lay still. Steele relaxed his grip. As he did so, Grantham's face contorted and his mouth opened wide.

"It's coming out!" Steele yelled to Bach.

Bach, wearing a pair of thick rubber gloves, moved closer to the table. Loengard stared in fascinated horror at Grantham's mouth. Two long, slimy tentacles shot out of the gaping hole. As Loengard watched, a hideous, crablike creature crawled into view. The creature's deadly looking tentacles waved in the air, as if searching for something.

"What is it?" Halligan screamed.

"It's a ganglion," Bach answered calmly.

The ganglion found what it was looking for—a new victim. In the blink of an eye, a tentacle whipped toward Steele, wrapping itself around the agent's right hand. Another tentacle quickly whipped around his neck, and before Steele had a chance to react, the ganglion was attached securely to the right side of his face.

Steele fell against the wall, clawing at the ganglion, trying to separate it from his face. It was useless. The creature's biggest, fattest tentacle inched toward his mouth.

"Get it off, get it off!" he screamed desperately. As he yelled, the ganglion's large tentacle slipped into his open mouth.

"It's trying to get inside him," Loengard yelled. He grabbed a pair of tongs from the table and raced toward Steele. With the tongs, Loengard took hold of the tentacle in Steele's mouth and began to pull. The creature thrashed wildly, trying to escape the tongs while still keeping a secure hold on Steele.

Bach stepped forward, brandishing a scalpel. While Loengard held the ganglion with the tongs, Bach sawed at the tendril that was burrowing deeper into Steele's head. Hurt, the creature released the agent completely. It writhed violently on the end of the tongs.

"Get that thing into the jar," Bach commanded Loengard, who stuffed the creature into the large glass container that Halligan had found. Bach quickly slammed the lid on and twisted it into place.

Imprisoned in the jar, the ganglion contorted violently, snapping its tentacles this way and that. *Crack!* The thing struck the side of the container so forcefully that the glass splintered. Within seconds, the creature would be free again.

"Move back!" Bach shouted. "Open the storage locker!" Bach grabbed the container and strode across the room. He placed the jar in a heavy steel refrigerator and slammed the door shut. From within the refrigerator came the sound of breaking glass, then a thud as the ganglion hurled itself at the door, trying to break free.

Popejoy entered the room with a locked metal box in his hands. He handed the box to Bach.

"Somebody mind telling me how that thing got inside Grantham?" Loengard asked.

"I don't know," said Bach. "But whatever that is, it's a dead ringer for this one here." He unlocked the metal box and pulled out a container. A dead ganglion floated in the clear preserving fluid inside.

"We found this fifteen years ago at the Roswell crash site. It was inside the body of the alien Gray you saw, Loengard," Bach said.

"Why wasn't the medical team told about any of this?" Hertzog asked.

"You didn't need to know," Bach answered, without a trace of remorse.

"Wait a minute," said Loengard. "You're saying you found one of these things in an alien . . . and now in a human being?"

Bach nodded. "Now there's only one question: How many more people like Grantham are out there?"

Chapter 10

Washington, D.C.

In Idaho, Bach had assured Loengard that everything back in Washington was under control, that he'd taken care of both Pratt and Kimberly for him. Loengard found out how the captain had "taken care" of Pratt when he finally returned to work.

The small, cluttered desk he had been stationed at was gone. Loengard had been moved into a real office, complete with walls, windows, and a large desk. His name had even been stenciled on the door.

Loengard entered and looked around, hardly believing his eyes. He stared out the window, enjoying his new view of the Capitol. He felt suddenly guilty. Mark Simonson had spent years working toward an office like this one.

Hearing the door open behind him, Loengard turned, expecting to see Simonson. Instead Pratt entered, closing the door firmly behind him.

"I hope the office meets your requirements, John," Pratt said. He looked at Loengard with cold fury in his eyes.

dark skies™

"Sir?" Loengard asked questioningly.

"'Sir.' Your slick line of garbage disgusts me," Pratt spat out. "You disappear for days with some flimsy lie for an excuse. I was all set to fire you. Then I find out that John Loengard is untouchable."

"What are you talking about?" Loengard asked, perplexed by Pratt's sudden change in attitude. He had thought the congressman liked him. What had happened?

"As if you don't know. Just blackmail, that's all." Pratt threw a stack of papers on top of the big, shiny desk.

Loengard flipped quickly through the papers. They contained medical information about Pratt. A small, typed note attached to the top page read, "Loengard's untouchable."

"Sir, I didn't—" Loengard began, but the congressman cut him short.

"So what if I had a nervous breakdown? I'm fine now," Pratt said. "But your friends release that, and Charles Pratt will never win another election. Who's behind all this, John?"

"All I can tell you is that I'm serving my country," Loengard replied, trying to sound sure of himself. He had some pretty serious doubts, though. How could Bach allow these kinds of tactics?

"You're serving your country by serving me up on a platter?" Pratt said. "I don't know who your friends are,

74

but I'll tell you something, *Mr.* Loengard. There are forces out there that are far more powerful."

Pratt turned and headed toward the door. Before leaving, though, he looked back at Loengard for one parting shot.

"Your girlfriend came by the office last week," he said. "Nice girl. She and I had a good long chat about you."

Great, thought Loengard. He reached for the phone and quickly dialed Kimberly's number at the White House.

"Kimberly Sayers."

"I'm back," Loengard said.

Kimberly's usually warm and friendly voice became suddenly frosty.

"John. How nice of you to call," she said.

"Listen, Kim—"

"No, you listen," Kimberly said firmly. "Why have you been lying to everyone? You told me you were out of town on business. You told Pratt your uncle died. John, you don't even have an uncle."

"I want to tell you everything, but it's just so complicated," Loengard said.

"You're going to uncomplicate things right now, or we're through," Kimberly said, her voice breaking. "I thought we were best friends. I thought we could tell each other everything."

Loengard paused. He knew he could never involve

Kimberly in this mess. "I can't tell you," he said. "Please just know that I—"

The phone had gone dead.

That evening, Loengard sat with Popejoy and Steele, watching Dr. Hertzog through the thick glass of the observation room. Hertzog was in the lab, drawing blood samples from a caged chimpanzee.

"They think by putting a piece of ganglion inside that monkey, they'll figure out how it works?" Popejoy asked skeptically.

"It didn't come with an instruction manual," Steele said.

"Yeah, but if you want to know how it works in humans, why fool with monkeys?" Popejoy asked. He obviously had some doubts about Majestic's tactics, too.

"You volunteering?" Loengard asked him, smiling.

"Not on your life," Popejoy answered. "My commitment to the cause goes just so far."

Hertzog entered the observation room. He carried a tray holding three vials of the chimp's blood.

"I'm taking these blood samples down to the lab," he said. "Probably too early for the monkey to begin behaving strangely, but keep an eye out."

After Hertzog left, Popejoy nudged Loengard. "What is this thing they've got you working on?" he asked, pointing to the pad Loengard was writing on.

"It's a report on Patient Zero. Grantham, the farmer," Loengard said. "Turns out the guy had a missing time gap, just like Betty and Barney Hill. Only his friends say he started acting crazy right after it happened."

"How many of these things do you think are out there?" Popejoy asked.

"One less than there used to be," Steele said, rubbing his throat. His neck still bore the marks of his confrontation with the ganglion.

"There's no way of knowing," said Loengard. "Not yet, anyway. You two have been at this longer than me. What do you think they want?"

Steele had heard enough. He wasn't about to answer questions for Bach's newest hotshot. He stood up and glared at Loengard. "How should I know?" he hissed. "Why don't you ask them?"

Popejoy and Loengard stared at each other after Steele left. Popejoy shook his head. "I don't know what they're after, but I'll tell you one thing," he said. "I don't think they care any more for us than old Doc Hertzog cares about those animals in there." He motioned toward the lab, where the chimp and the other experimental animals were kept.

Loengard glanced through the observation window. He bolted from his chair. "Popejoy, the chimp's gone!" he shouted. In the few short minutes the men had been talking, the animal had somehow gotten out of its cage and disappeared.

"We've got to get that chimp back in its cage," Popejoy said. "The captain'll kill me if that thing escapes."

"I'll take care of it," Loengard said. "You go get Hertzog and Steele."

Loengard stepped into the lab room and looked around. There were just two ways the monkey could have gotten out—through the observation room or through a second door that opened into the hallway.

He knew the chimp hadn't come through the observation room door, and he was pretty sure that the hall door was locked from the outside. The chimp must be hiding in here somewhere.

Loengard kneeled down to examine the cage where the chimp had been. There, on the floor, lay the combination lock Hertzog had placed on the cage. The lock was open.

A feeling of dread surged through Loengard. The monkey must have figured out the combination and let itself out of the cage!

At that instant, Loengard heard something move directly above him. He tried to back away from the cage, but it was too late. Whatever the chimp carried was big and hard. The last thing Loengard remembered was a sharp pain in his head and an inky blackness washing over him in waves.

Chapter 11

Loengard awoke moments later, his head throbbing. Hertzog knelt beside him.

"Are you all right?" the doctor asked.

"The chimp—" Loengard tried to sit up, but pain shot through his head like tiny lightning bolts.

"It's okay; we got him," Steele yelled from the hallway.

"Not before he got Popejoy," Hertzog said, looking sadly at Loengard.

Loengard quit trying to sit up. He lay back down and covered his face as tears welled up in his eyes. Popejoy had been a good friend. He had tried to make Loengard feel like part of the team right from the start.

Now there could be no doubt: Wherever they came from, whatever they wanted, the ganglions were extremely dangerous.

Loengard spent the rest of the evening out walking. Around three in the morning, he found himself by the

Reflecting Pool, staring at his own reflection. Today had been the darkest day of his life. First Kimberly, now Popejoy—both gone. How had things gotten so out of control?

Bach had said that the truth came at a great cost. But Loengard had never imagined the truth was going to cost him everything he cared about.

A bright, swiftly moving light streaked across the dark sky. Seeing its image reflected in the black waters, Loengard shuddered. Just a few short months ago, he would have thought it was a shooting star. He and Kimberly would probably have made a wish on it.

Loengard lowered his head and sobbed out loud. At that moment, he would have given anything to return to the warm, bright days of ignorance.

Chapter 12

Kimberly Sayers tossed and turned for hours before finally falling asleep. She had been so sure that John would have a good explanation for his strange behavior. She had been certain that the two of them would be able to work together to take care of whatever was going on.

How could I have been so wrong about him? The thought burned in her brain before she finally drifted into a troubled sleep.

Now Kimberly was awake again, startled out of sleep by a loud noise outside, like something breaking. She glanced at the clock, then climbed out of bed and trudged drowsily across the floor to investigate.

Out on the patio, Kimberly looked up into the sky. There, about a mile above her, a strange, bright light hovered in the darkness. The light filled her with fear and disgust. Hurrying inside, she firmly closed the doors behind her.

Kimberly turned back toward her warm bed and then

stopped in her tracks. Any trace of sleepiness vanished. Her eyes widened at the sight before her.

Two creatures with huge heads and big black eyes stared back at her. One was directly in front of her. The other stood in front of the doorway to the living room, blocking her escape. Finding her voice, Kimberly screamed. The creature near the door opened its tiny mouth and made a strange mewling sound. It was trying to mimic her scream, Kimberly realized.

The thing closest to her held up its hand as if to quiet her. Its long, sticklike fingers grasped a strange brown sac. The sac looked like a small hornet's nest. The creature squeezed the sac. A thick, milky liquid oozed out, forming a small puddle on the floor.

Kimberly watched, frozen and helpless, as the puddle began to move, gliding rapidly across the floor toward her. It spilled over her toes and began climbing up her legs. It moved quickly, completely covering Kimberly in a milky film. She opened her mouth to scream once more, but no sound came out.

The patio doors flew open, and a cold, bright light shone in on the scene in the bedroom. Slowly Kimberly's cocooned form was drawn up into the light. The creatures in the bedroom followed, and the light vanished as quickly as it had come.

Loengard stood in front of Kimberly's door. He had been tempted to come here last night, to tell Kim everything that had been going on. He had finally decided against it, however. He was willing to let Kim go if he could keep her safe from the terrible knowledge he now had.

He had decided that he just needed to talk to her He had waited outside the apartment for an hour, hoping to catch her on her way to work. She hadn't come out.

Loengard knocked loudly. Kimberly finally answered the door. She looked terrible. "John, I feel so sick," she said, looking up at him.

"Come on, let's get you back into bed," Loengard said, helping her toward the bedroom. Kimberly leaned on him heavily, clutching her head with one hand.

After settling Kimberly in bed, Loengard closed and locked the open patio doors. He sat on the edge of the bed and held Kim's hand, gently pushing the hair back from her face.

"Look, I'm sorry about yesterday," he said. "I just want you to know—I'm into something that I'm going to try to get out of. Please don't leave me, Kim. I love you."

"All right," Kimberly said. "I'm so tired."

Loengard kissed Kimberly's forehead. "Feel better," he said. "I'll call your office, let them know you'll be out today."

After he left, Kimberly lay in bed, trying to remember—what? She didn't know. She felt sick, confused, and scared.

Suddenly Kimberly sat up quickly, touching her finger to her nose. Blood! She looked at her pillow and saw a large bloodstain there.

"What's happening to me?" she cried softly.

Chapter 13

Loengard swallowed nervously and looked at the twelve men seated around the table. They stared back at him. He recognized some of the men as people he had seen on TV or in the newspapers—famous war heroes, diplomats, and politicians.

The men were the directors of Majestic 12, and they were waiting to hear what he and Dr. Hertzog had to say. Loengard hit the switch of the film projector. Everyone watched as the chimpanzee that had killed Popejoy unlocked its cage and let itself out. The chimp climbed into the rafters overhead and began unscrewing one of the pipes there. Then it sat and waited.

Loengard turned away. He didn't want to watch the rest.

Dr. Hertzog began to speak. "After repeated viewing of the film, we now believe the so-called Grays may be nothing more than host bodies for the ganglions, much more intelligent creatures," he said.

The doctor waited until the men had seen the bloody

ending of the monkey film, then continued. "Once the alien parasite is introduced to a human host body, it attaches itself to the part of the brain stem that controls our emotions," he said.

"We think that humans who become hosts for the ganglions begin to display some very distinct behaviors," Loengard continued. "Like this woman here."

The men once again turned their attention to the screen. The film showed Loengard sitting across from a middle-aged woman with short brown hair. The woman looked extremely nervous.

"We know this woman visited her sister in Midland, Virginia, when there was an Air Force–documented UFO sighting there," Hertzog said. "But let's watch the film."

On-screen, Loengard was trying to get information from the woman. "The government's very interested in two calls you made to a farmer in Boise, Idaho, named Elliot Grantham," he said.

"I told you. He was just a friend of the family," the woman said. She fidgeted impatiently in her seat. "How much longer?"

Loengard's questions now took a strange twist. "So, Hilary, do you and your husband go dancing very often?" he asked.

The woman's reaction was even stranger. She jumped from her seat and stared angrily at the young Majestic agent. "We do not twist the night away on 'American Bandstand,' if that's what you mean," she yelled. She sank back into her chair. "He likes sports," she said, tears welling in her eyes.

The men around the table murmured. The woman's emotions were completely mixed up. She had shown extreme anger and sadness in response to the most normal questions.

On the screen, Loengard continued his odd line of questioning. "Sports? So when was the last time you had a spider mite burrow into you during a golf match?" Loengard asked.

Hilary thought about the question for a long time. Then she said, "He plays golf; I don't."

"Okay. At home then?" Loengard asked.

Hilary laughed happily. "You know, from time to time, I guess," she said. Her face became suddenly anxious. "We almost done?"

Captain Bach rose from his seat and switched off the film projector. "We still have a lot of questions about the ganglions," he said. "Such as, how do they get inside a host? How long does the takeover phase last? Who are their targets and why? What is their plan? All we have are questions and no answers."

"Do we still have that woman in custody?" one of Majestic's directors asked.

"Yes, she's under observation . . . " Loengard began, but Bach held up his hand.

"We attempted a cerebral eviction on her last night," Bach said.

"A what?" asked the director.

Loengard stared at Bach, shocked. "Why wasn't I informed?" he asked.

Bach ignored Loengard's question and looked at the director. "We tried to remove the ganglion through surgery. The patient did not survive."

A number of the directors jumped to their feet. "Experimenting on housewives and farmers!" said one. "I don't agree with this!" The directors began talking and arguing loudly.

Loengard turned angrily to Bach. How could Bach have ordered a cerebral eviction without telling him? He was an important part of this investigation.

Just then, a uniformed guard entered the room and presented an envelope to Bach. Bach opened the envelope, read the note inside, then turned to Loengard and Hertzog. "I'm afraid I'm going to have to ask you two to leave the meeting right now," he said.

Outside the room, Loengard confronted Hertzog. "Doctor, I don't understand," he said accusingly. "You told me you were working on *another* way of getting the ganglion out of its human host. Something about injecting the ganglion with a substance that would kill it and save the human."

"Listen to me," Hertzog said. "The alien rejection technique is nowhere near perfected. In theory, yes, the ART should work when performed on the larger brains of humans. But so far, all I've got to show for my experiments are several dozen dead laboratory rats."

"What we're doing just seems so wrong," Loengard said. His doubts about Bach and Majestic nagged at him even more strongly than before.

"Some advice, John. Put your emotions aside." Hertzog patted Loengard on the back. "We must stay focused on the task at hand."

Loengard nodded unhappily, then turned away from the doctor and headed down the hallway. Right now, all he wanted to do was see Kimberly and then go home.

Hertzog watched the young man leave. He shook his head. The doctor knew that Loengard was smart, capable, a good agent. But he just didn't seem hard enough or cold enough for the job. He would have to talk to Bach: Loengard's sensitivity could cause trouble for Majestic down the road.

Chapter 14

Washington, D.C.

When Loengard arrived at Kimberly's apartment, he found a crowd of people gathered in front of the appliance store next door. They stood clustered together, watching President Kennedy on three TVs in the big showroom window. Kimberly was among them.

"What's going on?" Loengard asked, putting his hand on Kimberly's shoulder. As she turned to look at him, he saw that her eyes were red and puffy.

"I don't know; it doesn't make any sense," Kimberly said. She gazed up at Loengard, confusion in her eyes.

A man standing next to Kimberly turned. He appeared pale and serious. "Looks like we're on the brink of a nuclear war," he said. "The Soviets have missiles in Cuba."

"War?" asked Loengard. How could this be? Didn't the President know that there was a more deadly enemy to be fought? Then it hit him. Kennedy didn't know! For some reason, the President of the United States had not been told about the ganglions.

Anger flared in Loengard. These ganglions were the most serious threat humankind had ever faced. Kennedy *needed* to know.

Loengard took Kimberly's hand and led her to her apartment. "I'll come by later," he promised.

He rushed back down the stairs and into his car. Bach had a lot of questions to answer.

By the time he got to Bach's house in Bethesda, Maryland, Loengard was furious. He banged loudly on the front door. When Bach opened the door and saw Loengard, his face hardened. He stepped outside, closing the door behind him.

"There is not a reason good enough to explain why you're here," he said. His voice was filled with cold anger. Every Majestic agent knew the rule: Never contact Bach at his home. Ever.

Loengard was not frightened. "Well, since the world seems to be going up in smoke, I thought we could bend the rules a little," he said sarcastically.

"What do you want, John?" Bach asked impatiently.

"I want the truth. I know the truth is always changing with you, but I want to know about this Cuban missile thing," Loengard said.

"I am under no obligation to discuss this with you," Bach said. He turned toward his front door.

"See, that's exactly what I'm talking about," said Loengard, raising his voice. "Whom exactly *are* you obligated to discuss this with? While I'm watching TV, I keep asking myself whether Kennedy has told the Soviets about the Gray you have in cold storage. Because if he had, I don't see how they could be threatening each other like this."

Bach turned back to Loengard. "You're scared, John," he said. "Why don't you leave? Go be with Kimberly. She's probably pretty scared, too."

"We're all scared," said Loengard. "You're the only one who's not."

"Don't worry, they'll work it out. They have to," Bach said.

"President Kennedy doesn't know about Majestic, does he?" Loengard asked. He already knew the answer, but he wanted to hear Bach say it.

Bach changed the subject. "I took a big chance taking you on board," he said.

"So I should be eternally grateful?" Loengard laughed bitterly. "Forget it. Not if I'm being lied to. Now it's a simple question, Frank. Does he know? Yes or no?"

Bach raised his eyebrows. He knew Loengard was persistent. That was one of the qualities Bach admired in the young man. Loengard would probably stand here all night until he got his answer. "President Kennedy knows what he needs to know," Bach said finally.

"I knew it!" Loengard said. "Just tell me this: Who appointed you God?"

"President Eisenhower," Bach replied, ignoring the sarcasm in Loengard's voice. "He gave us the authority to decide which future presidents should be told. It's all perfectly legal."

"It might be legal, but it's wrong," said Loengard. "You don't keep the President of the United States in the dark about this."

"Look at the panic this whole Cuba thing's caused," Bach said. "How do you think people would react if they learned about the ganglions?"

Loengard considered Bach's question. Finally he said, "You know, Frank, if you're going to fight for humanity, then at least have a little faith in us."

Loengard turned and headed back to his car. Bach continued to stand outside long after Loengard had driven away.

Chapter 15

Kimberly wandered through her apartment in a daze. One minute she was in the kitchen, staring into the refrigerator. The next minute, she found herself in the living room, staring out the front window at the panicked crowd below.

Kim thought she remembered talking to John, but she couldn't be sure. She really couldn't remember much of anything. What was happening to her?

Hearing a strangely familiar buzzing sound outside her door, Kimberly cocked her head to one side. *It is waiting. I must let it in*, she thought as she crossed to open the door.

Pratt stood in the hallway. Without waiting for an invitation, he stepped inside.

"Hello, Kimberly," he said. "You've been expecting a visit. Your confusion is understandable. I'm here to help."

Kimberly backed fearfully away from him. "I don't want your help," she said.

Pratt closed the door and followed the young woman into the apartment. "I must say something to you now,

Kimberly," he said. "Are you ready to hear it?"

The sound was louder, stronger now. Searing pain ripped through her head. Kimberly clutched her ears. "That noise," she cried. "Make it go away."

"Listen. You have been chosen to watch John Loengard," Pratt continued. "He can no longer be trusted."

"No, no, no!" Kimberly shook her head violently, her ears still covered. "I won't do it. Leave us alone."

She watched as Pratt moved to the window and held his hand out, palm up. Hundreds of tiny lights shimmered through the closed windowpanes, moving in a beam to rest in Pratt's palm. The lights pressed together until they formed a small globe. The globe pulsated, changing from blue to purple to red to green. It was beautiful, but Kimberly was terrified of it.

Pratt advanced toward Kimberly, holding the light out to her. "Go ahead, touch it," he urged. "It will answer all your questions. Just reach out and touch the light. Then you'll be one of us."

Kimberly stared. She knew that if she touched the light, something very bad would happen. She also knew that touching the light would end the pain she felt. Kimberly reached out, stretching to touch the light.

An image of John flashed through her head. She dropped her hand quickly, as if burned by the nearness of the light.

"No! I won't! I won't!" she yelled at Pratt. She backed away from him but found herself up against the wall.

Pratt stepped ever closer. "It's natural to fight it," he said. "By now, you know where this must end. There is no escape."

His voice suddenly changed to a hoarse, raspy buzz. *"Klaar si su haar,"* he said in a language Kimberly had never heard yet immediately understood.

She stopped struggling and once again reached toward the light. Distantly, as if from another planet, she heard the sound of John's footsteps bounding up the stairs. With her last bit of free will, she pulled away from the light, turning her face to the wall to avoid looking at it.

"No!" she screamed.

Pratt sensed that Loengard was nearing Kimberly's door. He dropped the globe. It exploded into a thousand tiny lights and immediately vanished. Pratt turned to greet his enemy.

"Hello, John," he said as Loengard burst through the door.

Loengard rushed to Kimberly's side and held her close. She collapsed in his arms, sobbing and shaking.

"What are you doing here?" he asked Pratt.

"I came by to check on you. With this Cuba business and all . . . " Pratt gestured outside.

Kimberly shook her head. "He's in my head, John,"

she said, crying. "Or—something is." Loengard looked at Pratt, his eyes wide.

"It's too late, John," Pratt said. "We have her. She is one with us now."

Pratt has a ganglion inside him! Loengard thought, horrified.

"No! No!" Loengard cried. "Why her? Why not me?"

"Be patient, John," Pratt said. "Your time will come soon."

Loengard let out a wounded cry and jumped at Pratt. The man struggled violently, trying to escape. He reached for Loengard's throat, but the younger man pushed him forcefully away. Pratt slammed against the window, then disappeared as the force of the blow carried him through the shattering glass and onto the sidewalk below.

Loengard forced himself to look out the gaping hole in the window. Pratt lay mortally wounded on the sidewalk. A woman who had been standing with the crowd in front of the appliance store rushed to help him. She kneeled next to him and tried to comfort him.

As the woman bent close to Pratt, he began to cackle insanely. Loengard watched, frozen in horror. Pratt's mouth opened wide, and his face began to twitch and distort. The woman, sensing something very wrong, shrieked and ran.

If you only knew, Loengard thought, watching the woman escape into the black night.

Chapter 16

Loengard grabbed a blanket from the couch and wrapped it around Kimberly. He hustled her out to the car and headed for Dr. Hertzog's house, driving as fast as he dared.

"John, what's going on? What's in my head?" Kimberly asked him.

Loengard took a deep breath and told Kimberly about Majestic, and how he had been drawn into the secret organization. Then he told her about Grantham. He told her about the thing that had been inside the farmer, and what had happened when it came out.

In the passenger seat, Kimberly moaned softly, holding her head in both hands. Loengard glanced at her pale face and the dark circles beneath her eyes. He knew the aliens had chosen Kimberly because of him. Now he had to make things right again.

Loengard pulled up onto the lawn in front of Hertzog's house. He jumped out, ran to the door, and began pounding on it with both fists.

"Dr. Hertzog! It's me, Loengard!" he shouted. He grabbed the door handle and shook the locked door fiercely.

Hertzog appeared at the door in his bathrobe, his face puffy and still full of sleep.

Loengard grabbed the doctor's arm. "They got to my girlfriend," he shouted. "She's in the car. We've got to take her to Majestic. You have to do an ART on her."

"That's impossible," Hertzog replied, pulling away from the distraught agent.

"Let's go, doctor. Now!" Loengard began dragging Hertzog across the lawn.

"No," Hertzog said, quietly but firmly. The man's tone made Loengard stop and stare at him.

"You know what will happen, John," Hertzog continued. "Majestic has made the collection of live ganglions the number one priority. If we bring Kim in, I will be forced to do a cerebral eviction on her."

"You mean you'll have to cut it out?" Loengard asked in disbelief. "That will kill her."

"I have no choice," Hertzog answered.

"Can we do the ART here?" Loengard asked desperately.

"No, John. Don't put me in this position," Hertzog said. His voice was soft and apologetic but with a hard edge. Loengard knew that, no matter how hard he begged, the doctor would not perform the ART.

Loengard grabbed the front of Hertzog's bathrobe and shook him furiously. "I'll do it myself," he said, propelling the man back toward his door. "You just tell me what I need to know. And you make it quick."

The two men entered Hertzog's house. The doctor provided Loengard with the supplies he needed and gave him a quick rundown on the procedure itself.

The agent raced from the house and climbed swiftly into the car. Loengard knew the longer the creature remained inside Kimberly, the stronger it would become. He dumped the tablets the doctor had given him into a glass milk bottle filled with water. The water instantly began to foam, frothing out over the top of the bottle.

Loengard offered the bubbling liquid to Kimberly. "Drink it," he said.

Kimberly stared at the bottle. "What is that?" she asked.

"Dr. Hertzog says this will raise the pH level in your body. That will help get this thing out," Loengard explained.

Kimberly suddenly panicked. "I thought we were going to that place where you work," she said, her voice rising.

"No, we can't go there, Kim," Loengard said. He tried

to keep his voice calm and reassuring. "We've got to go find someplace else and do it on our own. Now come on and drink."

Kimberly looked down at her hands in her lap. Tears filled her eyes. "My hand. It won't move," she said.

Loengard placed the bottle in her hand, closing her fingers around the glass neck. Then he guided the bottle up to her mouth. "You have to fight this while you're still in control," he said.

Kimberly's raised hand shook with the effort. "It's too hard, John," she said.

"Drink it," Loengard replied. "It will help, I swear to you."

Kimberly managed to get the bottle to her lips. She took two big gulps, then dropped the bottle. Her hands shot to her head, squeezing tightly.

"Oh, no!" she cried. "It's moving in my head! It's moving in my head, John!"

Loengard started the car and sped off into the night. After driving around for nearly half an hour, he spotted a boarded-up house with a *For Sale* sign in the front. "This will work," he said. "No one will find us here." He helped Kimberly out of the car and around the back of the house. He gave the back door a powerful kick, sending it flying open.

The inside of the house looked no better than the

outside. It was a filthy place, dark and depressing. *It will have to do*, Loengard thought.

In the living room, two battered chairs and a table remained. Loengard helped Kimberly sit, then unpacked the paper bag full of the materials Hertzog had given him. He took out a syringe and filled it with a clear solution.

"What is that?" Kimberly asked. Loengard glanced at her. She looked terrified.

"It's a special solution Dr. Hertzog has come up with," Loengard said. "I have to inject the ganglion with something that will attack it. Then, with your pH off balance, it will want to leave your body."

"What happened to the other people he did this to?" Kimberly asked. "And no more lies."

Loengard approached Kimberly with the syringe. "It has never been tried on a person," he said.

"So unless I want to live with it . . . " Kimberly began.

"You *can't* live with it, Kim," Loengard said. He walked behind Kimberly and pushed her hair away from her neck.

At Loengard's touch, Kimberly jumped out of the chair, knocking him backward. She raced toward the front door. Finding it locked, she scratched and clawed at it, whimpering strangely.

Loengard tackled his girlfriend, but she had the strength of three men. She lashed out, opening a cut above his eye with her fist. Loengard held on. He was finally able to grab her flailing arms and pin them behind her. He sat on top of her, once again pushing the hair away from her neck.

Kimberly bucked and kicked wildly, but this time Loengard accomplished his task. He pushed the needle in and emptied the solution into her body.

Kimberly went limp. Loengard picked her up and put her back in the chair. He looked around the old house until he found some extension cords in the basement. He took the cords upstairs and tied his girlfriend securely to the chair. With the creature inside Kim controlling her actions, he could take no more chances.

Loengard pulled up the other chair next to Kimberly and waited. As the hours wore on, sweat broke out on Kimberly's face. She became even paler than she had been before. Every so often, she would make a small, soft noise and twitch in her seat, straining against the bonds that held her in place.

More than ten hours later, Kimberly remained unconscious. "It's not working," Loengard said softly, stroking Kim's clammy forehead.

Kimberly began muttering in some strange, unknown language, repeating one phrase over and over.

Loengard shook her. "Kim, it's me, John," he said. "Everything's going to be okay."

Kim looked up at him. She sat up straight in the chair. "You have to let me go, John," she said clearly and calmly.

"Not yet," Loengard replied.

"I'm okay," Kimberly said, speaking slowly and convincingly. "It worked. Really."

"Not yet, Kim," Loengard said. "I'm sorry, I just can't . . . "

Kimberly's face twisted with rage. "I hate you!" she screamed, spittle flying from between her parched lips. "You let me go!"

"That's not you talking. Please, Kim, keep on fighting it," Loengard said.

Now the thing inside Kimberly tried a different approach. "Honey, please, I just want to go home," she said, her voice soft and pathetic. "I feel sick, John. Just take me home to my own bed. Please, just take me home."

Loengard couldn't stand it anymore. He turned from Kimberly, covering his ears with his hands. Behind him, she kept on pleading, breaking into loud sobs. When would this ever end?

Suddenly Kimberly was silent. Loengard spun around. She sat with her head thrown back, her eyes rolling sightlessly. Her mouth opened and closed, but no sound came out.

All at once, Kim leaned forward and made a gagging noise. A ganglion flew from her mouth and landed on the floor in front of her.

The creature was smaller and less developed than the one that had come out of Grantham. It lay on the floor, its tentacles limply flopping this way and that. Loengard crushed the thing with his heel.

This one's not being taken alive, he thought, grinding the creature into the floor.

When he had finished, Loengard turned to his girlfriend. "It's over, Kim," he said.

But Kimberly didn't respond. She didn't seem to be breathing at all. Loengard quickly began to untie her motionless body from the chair.

Chapter 17

Once more, Loengard hurriedly bundled Kimberly into the blanket. He carried her outside and placed her gently in the backseat of the car. As he shut the door, four dark figures emerged from another car parked across the street. Loengard knew immediately who they were.

"So you couldn't help me, but then you go running to them?" he said accusingly to Dr. Hertzog.

"Please, John," Hertzog said. "I know how you feel, but it's my job."

Loengard turned to Bach. "Frank, if you're going to follow me, why don't you at least help?" he said.

"We just got here," Bach replied. "We had to clean up the mess you left at the apartment."

"I'll bet you knew about Pratt all along," Loengard said.

Bach ignored the comment. "We need Kim's body. Don't let her death be in vain, John," he said.

"You guys are like vultures," John said bitterly. "The only problem is *she's not dead!*"

Loengard sat by Kimberly's bedside, holding her hand while she napped. He hadn't left her since arriving at Majestic.

Hertzog and Bach watched the two through the thick glass of an observation window. The girl's survival had surprised Hertzog. She had gone through a terrible ordeal.

Hertzog was also surprised that Loengard had been able to carry out the procedure. *Maybe Loengard is tougher than I thought.* Hertzog spoke quietly to Bach, then walked away.

Bach tapped at the window and motioned to Loengard. He kissed Kimberly on the head and left her to sleep.

"You can take her home tomorrow," Bach said. "If she starts remembering any details, I want her brought back immediately."

Loengard nodded. He looked through the glass at Kimberly, who was sleeping peacefully. *I almost lost her,* he thought miserably.

"I want out," he said, turning back to face Bach.

"You know I can't agree to that," Bach said.

"What am I supposed to do? How am I going to explain all of this to Kimberly?" Loengard asked.

"That's your business. My business is to keep you on the team," Bach replied.

"I'm twenty-five years old. I'm nobody. You don't need me," Loengard said. He knew that if he couldn't persuade Bach to let him out now, he would never be able to.

"Look, John, why don't you take a break? Get your life in order," Bach suggested. "Just remember, you work for us, always. That part never changes."

Loengard watched Bach turn and walk away.

At that moment, Loengard knew that, like it or not, Majestic would be part of his life until the day he died.

Chapter 18

November 1963
Bethesda, Maryland

Loengard and Kimberly sat in a car down the block from Bach's house, watching Bach and his wife kiss their children as they went off to school.

Loengard looked at his girlfriend. "Are you sure you want to do this?" he asked.

"We have to, John," she replied. "People have a right to know about this."

After Kimberly had come home, Loengard had told her everything—about the ganglions, the Grays, and Majestic. Together they decided that people were entitled to know about the danger they were in. They spent months working on a plan to tell the President everything they knew.

First, however, they needed proof. Smuggling anything past Majestic's supertight security was impossible. So they had decided to break into Bach's house to get what they needed. For weeks, the two had studied the captain's routine. Now they were ready to make their move.

Kimberly donned a pair of sunglasses and pulled a colorful scarf around her head. She walked briskly up to the front door and rang the bell. Mrs. Bach answered.

"Hi. I'm sorry to disturb you this early in the morning. My name is Charrise Rich," Kimberly said, smiling brightly. "I'm a substitute teacher at Willow Elementary."

"Yes?" said Mrs. Bach.

"I've got the directions to the school, but I must have taken a wrong turn. Can you help me?"

As Kimberly engaged Mrs. Bach in conversation, Loengard quickly climbed up a large oak tree growing beside the house. He slid open a hallway window and climbed inside.

Moving quickly and quietly down the hall, he stopped in front of a closed door. Inside, Bach's singing carried over the sound of the running shower.

Loengard opened the door and peered into the bathroom. There it was! The box that Bach wore constantly around his neck—except when he showered—sat on the counter near the sink.

Loengard reached in and picked up the necklace. He slid the lid open, grabbed Bach's souvenir from the Roswell crash, then quickly closed the lid. He placed the necklace carefully back on the counter, trying to make sure he left it exactly as Bach had.

He made his way back down the hall and out through

the window. On the ground, he ran to the car and climbed in. One quick honk of the horn let Kimberly know that he had finished safely.

At the sound, Kimberly glanced at her watch. "Goodness, look at the time," she said. "If I don't get a move on, they're going to need a substitute for *me*! It was nice meeting you, Mrs. Bach."

Mrs. Bach waved and closed the door.

Kimberly rushed back to the car, opening the driver's-side door. "We did it!" she said excitedly.

Loengard was more somber. "We've finished part one," he said. "Part two depends on you. Are you ready?"

Kimberly swallowed nervously. "Ready," she said. She turned the key in the ignition and began the drive back to Washington, D.C. Back to the White House.

Chapter 19

Washington, D.C.

Kimberly tried to appear confident as she entered the executive reception area of the White House. She clutched a large manila envelope in her hands.

"Mrs. Lincoln? Hi. I'm Kimberly Sayers. I work for Alicia Burnside," she said, smiling at President Kennedy's secretary.

"Yes, I remember seeing your name on the staff list," said Mrs. Lincoln. "How can I help you?"

"Umm, Mrs. Kennedy would like the President to review the Hyannisport redecoration plan," she said, holding up the envelope.

"Here. I can attach it to his daily briefing." Mrs. Lincoln reached out to take the envelope.

Kimberly took a step backward. "Mrs. Kennedy told me to make sure only the President saw it," she said. She offered a weak smile of apology.

Mrs. Lincoln reached out again. "Don't worry, my dear. If I've learned one thing in all these years, it's to let the wives call their own shots," she said dryly.

"I'll see to it that the President gets it alone."

"Oh, thank you," Kimberly said. She breathed a huge sigh of relief. "I'm sure that'll be really appreciated."

She watched as Mrs. Lincoln took the envelope into the Oval Office and handed it to the President. She and John had done as much as they could. Now they would have to wait and see what would come of their efforts.

The two didn't have long to wait. In less than a week's time, Loengard found himself in a big black limousine, on his way to a meeting with Attorney General Robert Kennedy, the President's brother.

The limo pulled up a long driveway and stopped in front of a huge front lawn full of trees. Kennedy and two aides watched from the porch of an immense mansion. As Loengard stepped from the limo, Kennedy moved across the lawn to welcome him.

"Mr. Loengard," he said. The two men shook hands.

"Sir. It's an honor," Loengard replied.

"The honor's mine. If what I'm beginning to believe is true, you've put a lot on the line to get here," Kennedy said.

"Well, sir, a lot is at stake," Loengard said.

Kennedy nodded at his aides. Then he took Loengard's arm and led him away from the mansion. When the two were out of sight of the others, Kennedy turned to him. "We had the sample analyzed," he said. "We also checked out certain elements of your story— very discreetly, of course. Everything seems to hold together. I have to tell you, concentrating on the day-to-day matters at hand has been rather difficult."

"What is the President going to do?" Loengard asked.

"The President has less than a year left in his term. He's got to get reelected if he's going to do anything," Kennedy said. "I think we can take care of this during his second term."

"And you'll get me out of Majestic, right?" Loengard asked hopefully.

"Sorry, John, you have to stay put," Kennedy said. "The President needs someone like you on the inside. You'll be contacted from time to time. Will you do this for us?"

Loengard nodded. He had hoped that the President could order Bach to let him go. But the important thing was that Kennedy now knew about the aliens and that he would act. Eventually Loengard would be free of Majestic.

The future was beginning to look bright again.

Chapter 20

Bach sat staring at the screen in front of him. Although there was no sound, Bach knew what was going on. Loengard had betrayed him.

There it was, in black and white: Loengard chatting with Bobby Kennedy; Kennedy patting Loengard on the shoulder; Loengard leaving in Kennedy's limousine.

Bach was enraged. He had brought Loengard on board. He had helped him along, taken him under his wing. He had told Loengard things about Majestic that he had told no other person. And now this.

Bach rose and turned to Steele, who stood smirking by the film projector. "You don't get to the Attorney General unless he wants you to. Unless he's already seen something incriminating," he said, as much to himself as to Steele. "What could it possibly be?"

Bach sat down and thought. There was no way Loengard could have taken anything from Majestic. Absentmindedly he fingered the chain around his neck. Then it hit him.

Ripping the chain from his neck, he opened the box. The triangle was gone! Bach roared and threw the box and chain at the screen, as if he could hurt the image of Loengard there.

Just one thought filled his head: Loengard would pay for this treachery.

Chapter 21

Loengard and Kimberly spent the evening at their favorite restaurant, celebrating. Then they headed back to Loengard's apartment to watch TV.

"Need a lift up the stairs?" Loengard asked. "I saw how much spaghetti you packed away tonight."

"Not funny, John," Kimberly said. She pushed him aside and ran upstairs, then down the corridor to his apartment. She stopped abruptly at the doorway.

"John, what does this mean?" Kimberly's voice shook with fear.

Loengard strode down the hallway and into his small apartment. Everything inside had been trashed. Pictures had been torn off the walls, the sofa had been slashed, drawers had been pulled out and emptied. He glanced briefly at the mess, then moved to the window.

Across the street, two men in black suits were getting out of a big, dark car. As the driver exited, his suit coat swung open, revealing a holstered gun.

"They're coming back," he said. "And they've got

guns." Loengard quickly formed a plan. He hid behind the doorway. Kimberly sat, waiting, in the middle of the room.

The two cloakers burst through the open door. One grabbed Kimberly roughly by her coat and pulled her to her feet.

"Where's Loengard?" he growled.

Loengard stepped from the shadows and hit the cloaker over the head with a lamp. The cloaker fell to the floor, unconscious.

Loengard turned to the second cloaker, who was struggling to pull his gun from its holster. Loengard hit him as well, knocking the man to the ground. Loengard grabbed his gun.

"Let's go," he said to Kimberly.

The two raced down the stairs and into the car. Loengard drove off into the night, his lights off. Two blocks later, he turned the headlights on, stepped on the gas pedal, and left Washington, D.C., as fast as he could.

Chapter 22

Norman, Oklahoma

Loengard and Kimberly drove for eighteen hours, stopping only for gas. Neither slept. By the time they got to Norman, Oklahoma, they were both exhausted. They found a small, anonymous motel and parked in the back. Then they went inside and collapsed.

Loengard slept for almost twenty-four hours. Kimberly drifted in and out of sleep. Waking at the slightest sound, she would jump to the window and peer furtively out from behind the dark, heavy curtain.

The next day, Loengard walked to a nearby convenience store and bought some food. When he came back, Kimberly was pacing from one end of the small room to the other.

"They know we told the President," she said. "There's no doubt about that. What are we going to do?"

"Well, we can't call anyone. Bach could be listening. Then he's got a road map straight to us," Loengard said.

At that moment, someone pounded on the door. The

two looked warily at each other. Could Bach have found them so quickly?

Loengard reached into his jacket and pulled out the revolver he had taken from the Majestic agent. He pointed the gun at the door and nodded to Kimberly.

"Who is it?" Kim shouted, approaching the door.

"It's the motel manager."

Kimberly opened the door a crack, just enough for her to peek outside and see the same small, mousy woman who had checked them in yesterday. The woman stood on the sidewalk, tears in her eyes, hugging herself tightly. "I just came by in case anybody hadn't heard," she said.

"Heard what?" Kimberly asked.

"Just turn on your TV," the manager said. She turned away. Kimberly watched her move on to the next room, pounding loudly on the door.

By the time Kimberly closed the door, Loengard had already snapped on the television. As the two listened to the news, Kim's hands flew to her mouth and she sank to the edge of the bed. Loengard stared at the screen in shock.

" . . . Kennedy died at approximately one o'clock, central standard time . . . today . . . here in Dallas. He died of a gunshot wound to the brain. I have no other details regarding the assassination of the President at this time."

Loengard sat next to Kimberly on the bed. He put his arms around her as she collapsed in tears. "We're all alone, Kim," he said.

The two left the motel immediately. They didn't know where they were going; they just headed west. They drove in silence for a while, the awful news of the President's death still sinking in.

"Who will help us now?" Kimberly said, breaking the silence.

"I don't know," Loengard replied. "But we have to try. We can't just sit back and do nothing."

"You're right, John," Kimberly said. "We can't let them win. We have to stop them."

John looked at Kimberly. He knew he should be sorry that he had pulled her into this mess. But he was incredibly thankful that she was with him.

"We have the thing they fear most," Loengard said. "The truth."

The two stared out over the vast, flat land that lay before them. Up ahead, the sky had become overcast and gray. They drove on, into the waiting storm.

Don't miss the next exciting

d a r k   s k i e s™

Alien Invasion

Will the alien plan succeed?

John Loengard and Kimberly Sayers are running for their lives. They know all about a top-secret government organization code-named Majestic that is trying to rid the world of aliens. But the aliens won't be stopped. In fact, they have a plan of their own.

The aliens have secretly been implanting themselves in the minds of humans. Lots of important people now have aliens in their heads—including someone at Majestic. And he's after John and Kimberly. Can they stop the alien invasion before it's too late?

ISBN 0-8167-4337-1

$3.95 U.S.
$5.50 CAN.

Available wherever you buy books.

VISIT PLANET TROLL

A super-sensational spot on the Internet

at http://www.troll.com

Check out Kids' T-Zone, a really cool place where you can...

- Play games!
- Win prizes!
- Speak your mind in the Voting Voice Box!
- Find out about the latest and greatest books and authors!
- Shop at BookWorld!
- Order books on-line!

And a UNIVERSE more of GREAT BIG FUN!